THE DRAGON'S MATE: THE CLAN BOOK 3

LEA LARSEN

© 2016

© COPYRIGHT 2016 BY: LEA LARSEN ALL
RIGHTS RESERVED
.
ALL RIGHTS RESERVED. NO PART OF THIS BOOK
MAY BE USED OR REPRODUCED
IN ANY MATTER WHATSOEVER WITHOUT

PERMISSION IN WRITING
FROM THE AUTHOR EXCEPT IN THE CASE OF

BRIEF QUOTATIONS
EMBODIED IN CRITICAL ARTICLES OR REVIEW.

TABLE OF CONTENTS

CHAPTER ONE .... - 4 -

CHAPTER TWO .... - 10 -

Chapter Three .... - 19 -

Chapter Four .... - 25 -

CHAPTER ONE

"THERE CAN BE NO QUESTION OF MATING THE GIRL NOW."

HIS MOTHER PACED BACK AND FORTH IN FRONT OF A LONG, CURTAINED WINDOW IN HER BEDROOM. IT WAS AFTERNOON. NEARLY A WEEK SINCE HIS BROTHER'S DEATH. SINCE THAT TIME, LLEWELLYN HAD SEEN ALANA ONLY ONCE. THE MORNING AFTER, HE WENT UP TO HER ROOM TO MAKE SURE THAT SHE WAS ALL RIGHT. SHE ASSURED HIM THAT SHE WAS.

"DON'T WORRY ABOUT ME," SHE'D SAID. "I CAN TAKE CARE OF MYSELF. YOU NEED TO LOOK AFTER YOUR MOTHER NOW."

IT WAS EASY TO PRETEND THAT WAS WHY HE HAD STAYED AWAY FROM HER ROOM. WHY HE HAD SENT ALL HER MEALS UP WITHOUT BRINGING THEM HIMSELF.

THE TRUTH WAS, HE WAS AFRAID TO FACE HER. AFRAID TO CONFRONT THE NEWS HE KNEW WAS COMING. AFRAID TO FACE WHAT HIS MOTHER WAS FINALLY TELLING HIM NOW.

"I DON'T SEE WHY NOT," LLEWELLYN SAID

quietly. His mother stopped her frantic pacing and stared at him with a fierce expression in her eyes.

"Don't you?" she asked. "The death of a clan member is no small thing. The death of your brother should not be taken lightly. Especially not by you."

"I don't take it lightly," Llewellyn said defensively. "But, I still say that Owain was the only one to blame for his death. He was the one who broke into Alana's room when both you and I had forbidden it. He was the one who tried to…"

He broke off, still unable to say the word. Unable to confront what nearly happened to Alana, what his brother nearly put her through.

"I know," his mother said more quietly. Understanding lacing her voice. "But the clan won't see it that way."

"If the clan needs someone to blame, then let them blame me," Llewellyn said desperately. "I'm the one who damaged Owain's wing. I'm the one who pushed him out the window. I should be punished for his death."

"You are the clan leader," his mother

SAID. "ALANA IS NOTHING MORE THAN AN AREFOL GIRL. THEY WOULD NOT THINK TO PUNISH YOU WHEN THEY SEE HER AS MORE THAN CULPABLE."

LLEWELLYN STOOD SLOWLY FROM HIS WOODEN CHAIR AND WALKED BEHIND IT. HE CLUTCHED THE BACK OF THE COLD WOOD, LOOKING DETERMINATELY AWAY FROM HIS MOTHER.
HE KNEW SHE WAS RIGHT. THE CLAN WOULD NOT LISTEN TO REASON. THEY WOULD NOT PUNISH THEIR OWN WHEN THERE WAS AREFOL BLOOD READY AND WAITING TO BE SPILLED.

NO, THE ONLY TWO OPTIONS LEFT FOR ALANA WERE DEATH OR A LIFE OF SEXUAL SLAVERY. THE LATTER WOULD BE SEEN AS PUNISHMENT ENOUGH. AND, THE MEN'S URGES WERE DESPERATE ENOUGH TO OVERLOOK THE DEATH OF A CLAN MEMBER.

IF SHE WOULD NOT AGREE TO BECOME A CONSORT FOR THE CLAN, AND LLEWELLYN WAS CONVINCED THAT HE WOULD NEVER, EVER ALLOW HER TO AGREE TO SUCH A PROSPECT, THE ONLY OTHER OPTION WAS DEATH. ON THE NIGHT OF THE FULL MOON, THE MEN OF THE CLAN WOULD EITHER HAVE THEIR LUST OR THEIR BLOOD LUST QUENCHED. THERE WAS NO AVOIDING IT. UNLESS…

"WHAT IF SHE DISAPPEARED BEFORE THE CEREMONY," LLEWELLYN SAID, LOOKING UP FOR THE FIRST TIME AT HIS MOTHER. SHE LOOKED AT HIM WITH HER MOUTH PURSED CLOSED.

"YOU KNOW THAT'S NOT POSSIBLE," SHE SAID. "THEY WOULD FIND HER."

"NOT IF SHE LEAVES DURING THE RITUAL," HE SAID. "NOT IF SHE'S ALREADY HALFWAY ACROSS THE SEA BY THE TIME IT'S FINISHED."

THIS TIME, HIS MOTHER'S EYES WENT WIDE, HER SKIN TURNED PALE. SHE SEEMED TO REALIZE NOW THAT HE WAS, TRULY SERIOUS ABOUT THIS.

"LLEW YOU...YOU COULDN'T," SHE SAID QUIETLY. "THEY ARE EXPECTING A GIRL. THEY WERE PROMISED AN AREFOL. IF YOU DON'T DELIVER HER…"

"I KNOW WHAT THEY'LL DO," LLEWELLYN SAID. "I'M WILLING TO TAKE THAT CHANCE."

HIS MOTHER STARED AT HIM FIXEDLY, HER EYES HARDENING WITH EACH PASSING MOMENT.

"I SEE," SHE SAID. "AND, I SUPPOSE YOU'RE WILLING TO ALLOW ME TO GO THROUGH THE

PAIN OF LOSING BOTH MY SONS IN ONE WEEK?"

LLEWELLYN ONCE AGAIN AVERTED HIS GAZE. THE TRUTH WAS, HE HAD THOUGHT OF THAT. HE REMEMBERED HIS MOTHER'S TEARS AFTER OWAIN DIED. THEY FELT WORSE THAN HER TEARS AFTER HIS FATHER'S PASSING. PERHAPS BECAUSE THERE HAD BEEN TIME TO PREPARE WHEN HIS FATHER PASSED. BUT, WITH OWAIN...

HE COULD NOT DENY THAT HIS MOTHER'S CRY AS HIS BROTHER FELL THROUGH THAT WINDOW STILL HAUNTED HIM. HE KNEW IT ALWAYS WOULD. ALL THE SAME, HE COULD NOT ALLOW ALANA TO PAY THE PRICE FOR IT.

"THERE'S NO OTHER WAY, MOM," HE SAID.

"I WARNED YOU," SHE SAID FIERCELY. "I WARNED YOU NOT TO LET YOUR PASSION FOR THAT GIRL CLOUD YOUR JUDGMENT AND THAT'S EXACTLY WHAT IT'S DONE."

"WOULD YOU RATHER SHE DIE?" LLEWELLYN ASKED. "WOULD YOU RATHER I HAD MORE BLOOD ON MY HANDS?"

"I WOULD RATHER YOU PUT THE NEEDS OF YOUR FAMILY ABOVE YOUR OWN," SHE SAID.

LLEWELLYN OPENED HIS MOUTH TO RETORT

but thought better of it. Arguing with his mother would do him no good. He would not change his mind and, he knew that she would not change hers.

"Mother," he said as gently as he could. "I'm going to get her out. No matter what you say. I'm not asking you to get involved. All I need is your promise that you won't tell the others."

Her eyes, as bright green as his own, flashed as her pale lips remained pursed in a frown.

"As that would force them to kill you more quickly," she said. "You can have my promise that I won't tell them." Llewellyn nodded as his mother turned away from him and back to the window which looked out to a plain meadow, the shadow of Mount Snowdon in the distance.
Recognizing his mother's signal that their conversation was finished, he turned to the door and left the room.

Now, all that was left to do was what only one week ago seemed unthinkable. He had to send Alana away. And with her, any hope either he or his clan had of a future.

CHAPTER TWO

ALANA STARED OUT THE WINDOW THAT MORNING AS SHE HAD DONE EVERY MORNING SINCE THAT NIGHT.

THOUGH LLEW HAD RESTOCKED HER LITTLE LIBRARY WHICH HAD BEEN DESTROYED, SHE FOUND THAT BOOKS COULD NO LONGER HOLD HER INTEREST. NEITHER, IT SEEMED COULD THE RUINED CASTLE OR THE LARGE GREEN CLIFFS THAT SURROUNDED IT.

WHEN SHE LOOKED OUT OF THE WINDOW NOW, SHE LOOKED DOWN ONTO THE DARK PATCH OF IVY WHERE THE BODY HAD FALLEN NOT ONE WEEK BEFORE. SHE STARED HARD AT THE PATCH AS THOUGH HER GAZE COULD MAKE IT WHAT IT WAS BEFORE. AN ORDINARY PATCH OF IVY AMIDST A DOZEN OTHERS.

PERHAPS IF SHE STARED LONG ENOUGH, IF SHE TRANSFORMED IT IN HER MIND, EVERYTHING ELSE WOULD CHANGE AS WELL. MAYBE SHE WOULDN'T KEEP SEEING OWAIN'S FACE LOOMING ABOVE HER WHEN SHE CLOSED HER EYES. MAYBE SHE WOULDN'T SHUDDER AT THE MEMORY OF HIS UNWELCOME HAND FORCING ITSELF INTO HER.

MAYBE, JUST MAYBE, IF SHE ERASED THE ENTIRE EVENT FROM HER MIND, LLEWELLYN WOULD COME BACK TO HER. MAYBE HE WOULD TAKE HER IN HIS ARMS AND TELL HER THAT SHE WOULD STILL BE HIS, NO MATTER WHAT ELSE HAD HAPPENED.

SHE HAD NOT SEEN HIM SINCE THE DAY AFTER. HE'D COME TO HER ROOM TO MAKE SURE THAT SHE WAS ALL RIGHT. WHEN SHE ASSURED HIM THAT SHE WAS, HE LEFT. AND THAT WAS THAT.

OF COURSE, SHE TOLD HERSELF, HE'D NEEDED TO TAKE CARE OF HIS MOTHER. SHE'D EVEN TOLD HIM THAT SHOULD BE HIS FIRST PRIORITY. IT WAS ONLY NATURAL THAT HE'D HEEDED HER ADVICE.

BUT NOW, IT WAS THE DAY OF THE CORONATION. AND, SHE STILL HAD NO IDEA WHERE SHE STOOD WITH LLEW. IF HER ROLE HAD CHANGED. AND, IF IT HAD, WHAT THAT ROLE MIGHT BE.

ABSENTLY, SHE RAN HER HAND ALONG THE WINDOWSILL AND LIFTED HER EYES FROM THE PATCH OF IVY. SHE SOUGHT OUT THE LARGE STANDING STONES IN THE MIDDLE OF THE RUINED CASTLE AND THOUGHT OF THE RITUAL.

LLEWELLYN WAS SUPPOSED TO TAKE A MATE TONIGHT. NOW, GIVEN WHAT HAD HAPPENED, SHE HAD NO IDEA IF HE WOULD. PERHAPS THE RITUAL WOULD NOT HAPPEN AT ALL.

EITHER WAY, SHE NEEDED LLEWELLYN HERE. IF THINGS HAD CHANGED…IF HE NO LONGER WANTED HER…SHE NEEDED TO HEAR IT FROM HIM.

ALANA JUMPED IN SURPRISE WHEN THE DOOR TO HER ROOM CLICKED OPEN. SHE TURNED AND HER EYES WIDENED TO SEE LLEWELLYN STRIDING INSIDE AS THOUGH HER THOUGHTS HAD SUMMONED HIM.

HE ISSUED NO GREETING BUT CARRIED A LARGE BROWN SUITCASE AND HASTILY THREW IT OPEN ONTO THE BED.

"LLEW, WHAT—"

"YOU NEED TO LEAVE," HE SAID.

SHE FELT HER HEART DROP IN HER CHEST, THE BLOOD DRAINING FROM HER FACE.

"LEAVE?" SHE ASKED BREATHLESSLY.

"THIS AFTERNOON. YOU'LL SNEAK DOWN THE BACK STAIRS INTO THE KITCHENS AT EXACTLY THREE O'CLOCK. THERE WILL BE NO ONE

THERE TO SEE YOU THEN."

WITHOUT LOOKING AT HER, HE HASTILY MOVED TO HER WARDROBE AND PLACED A PILE OF CLOTHES ON THE BED. SHE MOVED SLOWLY TOWARDS HIM.

"BUT...BUT WHAT ABOUT THE CEREMONY?" SHE ASKED.

"DON'T WORRY ABOUT THAT," HE SAID. "I'LL HANDLE IT ON MY OWN. YOU HAVE TO GET OUT."

"YOU...YOU SAID THEY WOULD FIND ME NO MATTER WHERE I WENT," SHE SAID, HOPING THIS ARGUMENT MIGHT STOP HIM IN HIS TRACKS. IT DIDN'T, HE CONTINUED TO RUSH ABOUT THE ROOM, SETTING THINGS ONTO HER BED SO THAT SHE COULD PLACE THEM IN THE LARGE SUITCASE.

"THE CLAN DOESN'T TRAVEL ACROSS THE SEA," HE SAID. "I'VE BOUGHT YOU A ONE-WAY TICKET TO NEW YORK. YOU SHOULD BE SAFE THERE."

SHE LOOKED AT HIM TRYING HER BEST TO THINK OF SOME OTHER ARGUMENT. SOME LOGICAL REASON FOR HER TO REMAIN HERE. THERE WAS NOTHING LEFT FOR HER OUT IN THE REST OF THE WORLD, SHE WAS SURE OF

THAT. NO MATTER WHERE SHE WENT NOW, SHE WOULD NEVER BE ABLE TO CALL IT HOME. NOT WITH LLEWELLYN AND THE MANNER AND THE RUINED CASTLE STILL IN HER MIND.

"WHAT IF I SAID NO," SHE TOLD HIM. "WHAT IF I SAID I DON'T WANT TO GO?"

THE FIRM RESOLVE IN HER VOICE MADE HIM STOP BESIDE THE BED. HE PUT BOTH HANDS BESIDE THE SUITCASE AND LOOKED DOWN AT IT AS THOUGH HOPING IT MIGHT PROVIDE SOME COMFORT.

"YOU HAVE TO, ALANA," HE SAID.

"NO, I DON'T," SHE SAID FIRMLY WALKING TOWARDS HIM. "I TOLD YOU I WANT TO BE YOUR MATE. AND I MEANT IT."

SHE TOUCHED HIS ARM GENTLY THEN TOUCHED HIS CHEEK FORCING HIM TO LOOK INTO HER DARK EYES.

HE HAD NOT SEEN THOSE EYES IN NEARLY A WEEK. NOW THAT HE LOOKED INTO THEM, HE REALIZED JUST HOW MUCH HE HAD MISSED HER. HIS HEART LEAPED IN HIS CHEST WHEN SHE PULLED CLOSER TO HIM.

"I DON'T CARE WHAT ANYONE ELSE HAS TO SAY," SHE SAID. "I'M NOT GOING ANYWHERE."

WITH THAT, SHE CLOSED THE GAP BETWEEN THEM AND PUT HER LIPS DESPERATELY ON HIS. IT TOOK ALL THE STRENGTH HE POSSESSED TO PUSH HER AWAY.

"ALANA," HE SAID. "THEY'LL KILL YOU."

HER EYES WIDENED AND HER FACE LOST A BIT OF ITS COLOR AS SHE STEPPED BACK.

"MEMBERS OF THE CLAN BEGAN CALLING FOR YOUR BLOOD AS SOON AS THEY HEARD WHAT HAPPENED," HE TOLD HER. "IF YOU DON'T LEAVE...IF YOU COME TO THIS RITUAL TONIGHT...YOU WON'T COME OUT OF IT ALIVE."

SHE STAYED VERY STILL IN HER SPACE BY THE WINDOW. HE COULD SEE RED FORMING AT THE CORNERS OF HER EYES, WATER POOLED INSIDE THEM, THREATENING TO FALL ONTO HER CHEEKS.

AGAINST HIS BETTER JUDGMENT HE WALKED TOWARDS HER AND TOOK HER HAND IN HIS.

"BELIEVE ME," HE SAID. "THIS IS THE ONLY WAY."

TWO TEARS CASCADED DOWN HER CHEEKS AS HE OPENED THE PALM OF HER HAND, BROUGHT IT UP TO HIS LIPS AND PLACED A DESPERATE KISS ONTO IT.

ALANA ONLY HAD A MOMENT TO SAVOR THIS FAREWELL BEFORE HE DROPPED BOTH OF HER HANDS AND RUSHED OUT THE DOOR AS THOUGH ASHAMED OF HIMSELF.

SHE STAYED THERE FOR A LONG WHILE, LOOKING BETWEEN THE DOOR WHERE LLEW HAD LEFT AND THE SUITCASE SITTING OPEN ON HER BED.

SLOWLY, SHE WIPED THE TEARS FROM HER EYES, MOVED TO THE OPEN SUITCASE, AND BEGAN TO PACK.

Chapter Three

At exactly three o'clock, Alana moved as quietly as she could down the dimly lit staircase. The back staircase was much narrower than the main winding one which led out of her bedroom. It was a chore to move both herself and her suitcase through it.

She finally managed to reach the door at the bottom of the stairs and twisted it open. It revealed a large, pristine looking kitchen with one wood-burning oven and two stoves.

Alana searched this room until, finally, she found the back door Llew had instructed her to leave from. As quickly as she could, she moved towards it.

"I'd a feeling he would send you out the back way."

Alana jumped and let out a small cry at the sound of the woman's voice. Slowly, she turned around to see a tall woman making her way towards her from an archway at the far end of the kitchen.

SHE KNEW FROM THE LONG BLONDE HAIR MIXED WITH GRAY AND THOSE BRIGHT GREEN EYES THAT THIS WAS LLEW'S MOTHER. SHE ALSO KNEW WHAT LLEW SAID ABOUT THE CLAN CALLING FOR ALANA'S BLOOD. PERHAPS HIS MOTHER WAS A PART OF THAT.

ALANA BACKED TO THE DOOR QUICKLY, HOLDING HER SUITCASE AGAINST HER AS A SHIELD.

"THERE'S NO NEED TO BE AFRAID," THE WOMAN SAID. "I WON'T HURT YOU. BUT I NEED TO SPEAK TO YOU QUICKLY. THERE'S NOT MUCH TIME."

"TIME FOR WHAT?" ALANA ASKED SLOWLY LOWERING HER CASE, HER EYES STILL NARROWED SKEPTICALLY.
"THE RITUAL WILL BEGIN AFTER SUNSET," MRS. COUCH SAID. "THE CLAN IS EXPECTING AN AREFOL GIRL TO BE THERE. IT DOESN'T MATTER TO THEM IF YOU ARE KILLED FOR OWAIN'S DEATH OR YOU'RE MADE A CONSORT. EITHER WAY, YOU MUST BE THERE."

"LLEW SAID—"

"LLEW IS WILLING TO TAKE THE PUNISHMENT FOR YOU," SHE SAID.

"THE PUNISHMENT?" ALANA ASKED. SHE FELT HER HEART BEGIN TO BEAT QUICKLY THINKING ABOUT WHAT THAT MIGHT MEAN.

"THEY WILL KILL HIM IF YOU'RE NOT THERE," THE WOMAN SAID.

ALANA FELT HER LEGS BEGIN TO GIVE OUT. SHE PLACED HER HAND ON THE KITCHEN WALL FOR SUPPORT.

"I KNOW HE WANTS TO PROTECT YOU," MRS. COUCH CONTINUED. "I KNOW WHAT YOU MEAN TO HIM BUT…I CAN NOT…I WILL NOT LOSE BOTH MY SONS."

ALANA LOOKED AT THE GROUND TRYING TO THINK OF A RESPONSE, OF SOMETHING SHE COULD SAY THAT WOULD MAKE SENSE. IT WAS STILL TOO MUCH TO PROCESS.

"THE TRUTH IS," MRS. COUCH CONTINUED. "IF YOU GO INTO THAT CIRCLE TONIGHT, I'VE NO IDEA WHAT WILL HAPPEN TO YOU. YOU MIGHT BE KILLED, YOU MIGHT BE GIVEN TO THE CLAN, LLEWELLYN MIGHT FIND SOMEWAY TO SAVE YOU. BUT, I KNOW WHAT WILL HAPPEN IF YOU ARE NOT THERE. I KNOW MY SON WILL DIE."

ALANA LICKED HER LIPS AS SHE LET MRS. COUCH'S WORDS SINK IN. LLEWELLYN KNEW THAT HE WOULD DIE IF SHE DID NOT ATTEND THE RITUAL. WHEN HE TOLD HER TO LEAVE, HE KNEW THAT HE WOULD HAVE TO PAY THE PRICE FOR HER. AND, WHAT'S MORE, HE WAS WILLING TO.

NOW, SHE HAD A CHANCE TO SAVE HIM. EVEN IF SHE DIED IN THE PROCESS, SHE REALIZED IT WAS WELL WORTH THE RISK.

SLOWLY, SHE LOOKED UP FROM THE FLOOR INTO THE EYES OF LLEW'S MOTHER. THE EYES THAT LOOKED SO MUCH LIKE HIS, AND NODDED.

"ALL RIGHT," SHE SAID. "I'LL GO TO THE CEREMONY."

Chapter Four

ALANA HAD BEEN DRESSED AND PREPARED IN MRS. COUCH'S OWN ROOM. IT WAS LARGER, SHE CLAIMED, THAN ALANA'S BED CHAMBER.

LLEW'S MOTHER HAD PLACED ALANA IN A LONG, WHITE, CHIFFON GOWN WITH BELL SLEEVES. A LONG, DARK BRAID ENCIRCLED HER HAIR AND A CROWN OF RED FLOWERS HAD BEEN WOVEN INTO IT.

ONCE THE OLDER WOMAN WAS SATISFIED, SHE LED ALANA OUT OF THE MANOR TOWARDS THE RUINED CASTLE. IN THE FADING LIGHT OF THE SETTING SUN, ALANA COULD SEE THAT MORE THAN TWO DOZEN PEOPLE WERE ALREADY GATHERED INSIDE THE RING OF STANDING STONES.

MRS. COUCH KEPT ALANA AT A DISTANCE. HIDDEN IN THE SHADOW OF THE MANOR.

"REMEMBER," MRS. COUCH SAID TO HER. "WHEN THE TIME COMES, YOU WILL WALK SLOWLY TOWARDS THE STANDING STONES. THE CLAN MEMBERS WILL MAKE WAY FOR YOU. WHEN YOU REACH LLEWELLYN, REPEAT THE PHRASE I'VE TAUGHT YOU."

"WNEUD GYDA MI FEL BYDDWCH YN," ALANA REPEATED CLUMSILY, THE WELSH WORDS FEELING STRANGE INSIDE HER MOUTH. LLEW'S MOTHER LOOKED AT HER CRITICALLY.

"CLOSE ENOUGH," SHE SAID FINALLY. "WHEN THE SINGING BEGINS, MAKE YOUR WAY TO THE STANDING STONES."

THEY WAITED WHAT FELT TO ALANA LIKE AN ETERNITY BEFORE THE SUN DIPPED BEHIND THE CLIFFS AND THE FULL MOON BEGAN TO RISE.

WHEN THE CHANTING BEGAN, SIMILAR TO WHAT SHE HAD HEARD ON HER SECOND DAY AT THE MANOR, BUT SOMEHOW VERY DIFFERENT, ALANA'S HEART BEGAN TO POUND INSIDE HER CHEST. ANXIOUS SHIVERS COVERED HER ENTIRE BODY AND SHE FELT ROOTED TO THE SPOT. SUDDENLY, SHE COULD NOT MOVE.

IT TOOK A SHOVE FROM LLEWELLYN'S MOTHER TO FORCE HER FEET FORWARD. SHE WALKED SLOWLY TO HER DESTINATION, FEELING VERY MUCH LIKE A SPOTLESS LAMB BEING LED TO THE SLAUGHTER.

WHEN SHE REACHED THE STANDING STONES, JUST AS MRS. CROUCH HAD SAID, THE CLAN

MEMBERS MOVED ASIDE FOR HER. WHEN THEY DID, SHE COULD SEE LLEWELLYN STANDING IN THE MIDDLE OF THE CIRCLE.

AS SOON AS SHE CAUGHT SIGHT OF HIM, HER HEART SETTLED. EVEN WHEN HIS FACE DRAINED OF COLOR AND HIS EYES WIDENED IN SHOCK, SHE DID NOT WAVER IN HER RESOLVE.

"ALANA, WHAT ARE YOU DOING?" HE WHISPERED WHEN SHE REACHED HIM. "I TOLD YOU TO LEAVE."

SHE DID NOT ANSWER BUT GAVE HIM A SMALL SHAKY SMILE. WHEN THE CHANTING REACHED ITS END, SHE DROPPED TO HER KNEES IN FRONT OF HIM, JUST AS SHE HAD BEEN INSTRUCTED TO DO.

"WNEUD GYDA MI FEL BYDDWCH YN."

ONCE SHE HAD UTTERED THE PHRASE, SHE LOOKED UP AT HIM HOPING THAT HE WOULD READ WHAT WAS WRITTEN IN HER EYES. HOPING HE WOULD REALIZE WHY SHE HAD TO DO THIS.

HE STARED AT HER A LONG WHILE AND ALANA FELT HER HEARTBEAT QUICKEN ONCE MORE.

FINALLY, HE GRASPED HER HAND IN HIS AND PULLED HER UP TO HER FEET. BEFORE SHE

KNEW WHAT WAS HAPPENING, HE PULLED HER IN FOR A SEARING, LUST FILLED KISS. THERE WERE SEVERAL YELLS AND WHISTLES FROM THE MEN IN THE CROWD. IT WAS CLEAR FROM THEIR CHANTS THAT THEY THOUGHT LLEW MEANT TO MAKE HER THEIR CONSORT.

WHEN HE PUSHED ALANA BACK FROM HIM, SHE STEELED HERSELF. SHE HAD PROMISED SHE WOULD ACCEPT WHATEVER FATE LLEW WISHED FOR HER. SHE HAD MEANT WHAT SHE SAID. SHE BELONGED TO HIM, BODY AND SOUL, WHATEVER THAT MEANT.

SHE TOOK A DEEP BREATH AS LLEWELLYN TURNED TO THE CROWD.

"THIS," HE SAID TO THEM IN A LOUD VOICE, "IS MY CHOSEN MATE."

THE CATCALLS AND WHISTLES STOPPED INSTANTLY. A TENSE, PREGNANT SILENCE FELL OVER THE CROWD. EVEN AS ALANA'S HEART JUMPED WITH JOY AT WHAT SHE HAD HEARD, SHE LISTENED TO THE SOUND OF DISAPPROVING WHISPERS FROM THE MEN AROUND HER.

"SHE BELONGS TO ME AND NO ONE ELSE MAY CLAIM HER," HE SAID. "I WILL PROVE THIS TO YOU NOW."

ALANA STOOD FROZEN AS LLEWELLYN MADE HIS WAY OVER TO HER. SHE REMEMBERED WHAT BEING MATED TO HIM MEANT. WHAT SHE WOULD HAVE TO DO.

SHE SWALLOWED HARD AND STEELED HERSELF ONCE AGAIN AS LLEWELLYN TOOK HER IN HIS ARMS AND KISSED HER FORCEFULLY.

THIS KISS WAS POSSESSIVE, CALCULATED AND HARSH. THERE WAS NOTHING WARM OR LOVING ABOUT IT. EVEN SO, ALANA OPENED HER MOUTH TO WELCOME HIM. SHE COULD FEEL THE MAN SHE DESIRED BEHIND THIS HARDENED FACADE.

HE PULLED AWAY FROM HER AND WHISPERED IN HER EAR.

"I CAN'T BE GENTLE IN FRONT OF THEM," HE SAID. "THEY NEED TO SEE THAT I AM IN CONTROL OF YOU. THEY NEED TO SEE THAT I AM A LEADER. DO YOU UNDERSTAND?"

HE PULLED BACK SLIGHTLY AND SEEMED TO WAIT UNTIL SHE NODDED HER HEAD 'YES'.

HE LOOKED AT HER ANOTHER MOMENT, EYES SOFT, AND NODDED IMPERCEPTIBLY BEFORE STEPPING BACK AGAIN. SHE COULD SEE THIS HARD, COLD FACADE CREEP OVER HIS FACE

ONCE MORE. AND, SHE UNDERSTOOD, HE WOULD BE PLAYING A ROLE FOR HIS AUDIENCE. SHE HAD TO PLAY HERS AS WELL.

"ON YOUR KNEES," HE SAID FIRMLY.

ALANA CAST HER EYES DOWN AND DID AS SHE WAS TOLD. SHE WATCHED AS LLEW SLOWLY UNBUTTONED HIS TROUSERS AND PULLED OUT HIS LONG, SLENDER MEMBER, ONLY HALF HARD.

HE PRESSED IT TO HER LIPS AND, LOOKING UP AT HIM, SHE UNDERSTOOD WHAT HE WANTED. TENTATIVELY, SHE LICKED HIS LENGTH BEFORE SLOWLY ENCOMPASSING HIM FULLY.

AS SOON AS SHE DID, HE PRESSED HIS HANDS INTO HER HAIR AND FORCED HER TO SUCK AND LICK HIM UNTIL HE WAS FULLY HARD AND HIS MEMBER WAS LACED WITH THE BEGINNINGS OF THICK JUICES.

SHE GASPED WHEN HE TUGGED AT HER HAIR AND PULLED HER HEAD UP. LOOKING INTO HIS EYES, SHE PULLED HER MOUTH AWAY FROM HIM AND ALLOWED HIM TO GRAB HER HANDS AND LIFT HER TO HER FEET.

"NOW, STRIP," HE SAID. "SLOWLY, SO THAT I CAN WATCH YOU."

SHE CAUGHT A GLIMPSE OF THE CROWD NOW MURMURING TO EACH OTHER AND, SUDDENLY, SHE COULD NOT MOVE. SHE HAD NEVER UNDRESSED, EVEN IN FRONT OF WOMEN BEFORE. SHE DID NOT KNOW HOW SHE WAS GOING TO REVEAL HERSELF TO A CROWD OF MORE THAN TWENTY-FOUR ONLOOKERS, MOST OF THEM MEN.

SHE GASPED WHEN A HAND GRABBED HARD AT HER WRIST, TWISTING IT. LLEWELLYN BROUGHT HER TO HIM, HIS EYES HARD.

"DO YOU WANT TO MAKE ME ANGRY?" HE ASKED.

"N-NO SIR," SHE SAID TIMIDLY.

"THEN DO AS I SAY," HE LET GO OF HER WRIST AND SHOVED HER TO THE MIDDLE OF THE CIRCLE. SHE LOOKED AT HIM AND HIS EYES SOFTENED. SHE COULD SEE THE FACADE FALLING AWAY.

KEEPING HER EYES TRAINED ON HIS, SHE SLOWLY REACHED BEHIND HERSELF AND UNTIED THE CLASP OF HER DRESS. JUST AS SLOWLY, SHE PUSHED THE DRESS OFF OF HER SHOULDERS AND ALLOWED IT TO SKIM OVER HER HIPS AS IT FELL TO THE GROUND.

LLEWELLYN STROKED HIMSELF JUST AS

SLOWLY AS SHE UNDRESSED. LAZILY RUNNING A HAND OVER HIS MEMBER AS HIS EYES ROAMED OVER EVERY INCH OF HER SMOOTH, TAN SKIN.

WHEN HER BRA AND PANTIES HAD BEEN DISCARDED, SHE SHIVERED AGAINST THE SLIGHT BREEZE IN THE AIR, VERY AWARE THAT SHE WAS STANDING COMPLETELY NAKED, COMPLETELY VULNERABLE IN FRONT OF THESE MEN.

"COME TO ME," LLEWELLYN SAID CROOKING HIS FINGER AND BECKONING HER TO HIM.

HE TOOK HER HAND AND LED HER TO THE BACK OF THE CIRCLE WHERE A ROUGH CHAIR CARVED FROM ROCK STOOD. LLEWELLYN TOOK HIS SEAT ON THIS THRONE AND, ONCE MORE, BECKONED ALANA TO HIM. SHE MOVED TO HIM AND STOOD BY HIS SIDE.

HE GRABBED HOLD OF HER WAIST AND FORCED HER MOUTH DOWN ONTO HIS ONCE MORE. ONCE MORE, HE MOVED HIS MOUTH TO HER EAR.

"DON'T BE AFRAID," HE SAID.

WITH THAT, HE GRABBED HOLD OF HER WAIST AND FORCED HER ONTO HIS KNEE. HIS MOUTH CLAMPED HARD DOWN ONTO HER NECK AS IT

SUCKED AND BIT AGAINST HER. HIS HANDS GROPED HER BREASTS ROUGHLY BEFORE MOVING BETWEEN HER LEGS.

SHE CRIED OUT WHEN HIS FINGERS FOUND HER CLIT AND BEGAN TO CIRCLE HER OVER AND OVER AND OVER AGAIN BRINGING HER TO THE BRINK OF ECSTASY THEN FALLING BACK.

"WHO DO YOU BELONG TO?" LLEWELLYN ASKED LOUDLY ENOUGH THAT THE CROWD, STILL WATCHING COULD HEAR. HE TOUCHED HER AGAIN JUST WHERE SHE WANTED, NEEDED TO BE TOUCHED.

"Y-YOU," SHE SAID DESPERATELY. "I BELONG TO YOU."

"WILL YOU EVER BELONG TO ANYONE ELSE?" HE ASKED. BEFORE SHE COULD ANSWER, HE TOOK TWO FINGERS AND SHOVED THEM ROUGHLY INSIDE OF HER.

"NO-NO. NO ONE ELSE," SHE SAID. HIS FINGERS MOVED INSIDE OF HER AND SHE CRIED OUT AGAIN AS HE HIT AGAINST HER DESIRE.

"OH, GOD!" SHE SAID. AS SOON AS SHE DID, HE REMOVED HIS FINGERS FROM HER AND SHE LET OUT A WHIMPER OF PROTEST. BUT, BEFORE HER HEART COULD SINK IN DISAPPOINTMENT, HE PULLED HER ROUGHLY BACK TO HIM AND

MOVED BENEATH HER.

BEFORE SHE COULD READY HERSELF, HE THRUST INSIDE OF HER WITH ALL THE STRENGTH HE HAD.

SHE CRIED OUT, FIRST IN PAIN. THE FOREIGN OBJECT MOVING AGAINST HER CAUSED A STABBING SENSATION IN PLACES SHE DID NOT EVEN KNOW SHE HAD.

SUDDENLY, HE REACHED AN ARM OUT TO COVER HER BREAST AND, BRIEFLY, SHE STOPPED MOVING.

"RELAX," HE SAID. "IT'S JUST ME. I'M HERE. I WON'T HURT YOU."

TAKING A DEEP BREATH, SHE TURNED HER NECK TO LOOK AT HIM. HIS EYES WERE SOFT AGAIN. SLOWLY, SHE NODDED HER UNDERSTANDING.

AS SOON AS SHE DID, HIS EYES HARDENED ONCE MORE AND HE BEGAN FORCEFULLY THRUSTING INTO HER. SHE TOOK A DEEP BREATH AND, FOR THE FIRST TIME, FELT AN INCREDIBLE, INDESCRIBABLE PLEASURE BEHIND THE PAIN.

LLEWELLYN WAS INSIDE OF HER. HE WAS PART OF HER. THAT THOUGHT ALONE CAUSED A

FLOOD OF WETNESS TO FLOW TO HER CENTER, EASING HIS THRUSTS. WHEN HE TOOK ONE HAND AND WRAPPED IT AROUND HER WAIST, SHE GASPED AS HE BEGAN, ONCE AGAIN TO FINGER HER CLIT.

"ONCE AGAIN, MY LITTLE AREFOL," HE SAID. "WHO DO YOU BELONG TO?"

THE PRESSURE BUILDING INSIDE OF HER FROM HIS POWERFUL THRUSTS MIXED WITH THE TANTALIZING TEASING OF HER CLIT WAS ALMOST ENOUGH TO RENDER HER SPEECHLESS. THEN, SHE LET OUT A SCREAM WHEN HIS FREE HAND SLAPPED AGAINST HER BOTTOM.

"ANSWER ME," HE GROWLED. "WHO DO YOU BELONG TO?"

"I BELONG TO YOU," SHE SAID BREATHLESSLY. "I'LL ALWAYS BELONG TO YOU."

"GOOD," HE PURRED. "NOW COME FOR ME, MY PRETTY LITTLE AREFOL."

WITH ANOTHER FLICK OF HIS FINGER AGAINST HER CLIT AND A FORCEFUL THRUST INSIDE OF HER, SHE CAME SCREAMING AND PANTING AND MAKING SOUNDS SHE DID NOT KNOW SHE COULD MAKE.

HE FOLLOWED SOON AFTER PRESSING HER FAST AGAINST HIS NAKED CHEST CURSING INTO HER EAR.

WHEN IT WAS DONE, HE HELD HER THERE FOR SEVERAL MOMENTS. SHE LISTENED TO HIS BREATHING AND FELT IT SYNC IN TIME WITH HER OWN. FINALLY, HE PRESSED A KISS TO HER NECK AND MOVED HIS LIPS TO HER EAR.

"I LOVE YOU," HE WHISPERED TO HER.

ALANA HAD NO CHANCE TO ANSWER BEFORE HE PUSHED HER FROM HIM, FOLDED HIS MEMBER BACK INTO HIS TROUSERS AND MOVED TO THE MIDDLE OF THE CIRCLE ONCE MORE.

"YOU ARE WITNESSES," HE SAID. "I HAVE TAKEN MY MATE. SHE IS MINE AND I AM HERS."

THERE WAS SILENCE WITHIN THE WAITING GROUP FOR WHAT SEEMED LIKE FOREVER. ALANA FEARED FOR A MOMENT THAT IT HADN'T BEEN ENOUGH. THAT THE CLAN WOULD DEMAND THAT THEY BOTH DIE.

THEN, OUT OF SOMEWHERE NEAR THE BACK, A VOICE CALLED OUT.

"SHE IS YOURS FOREVER!"

MORE VOICES SLOWLY BEGAN TO REPEAT THE SAME MANTRA. ALANA LOOKED UP AT LLEWELLYN, WHO, APPARENTLY SATISFIED, SMILED DOWN AT HER.

THEN, QUICKLY, HE MOVED HIS HANDS BENEATH HER AND PICKED HER UP IN HIS ARMS AS THOUGH SHE WERE A BRIDE ON THE WAY TO HER HONEYMOON SUITE.
THE GROUP FELL SILENT AS THEY LEFT THE SAME WAY ALANA HAD ENTERED. WHEN SHE EXITED THE CIRCLE, SHE HEARD A LOUD CRY OF JUBILATION AND SOON, LAUGHING VOICES AND MUSIC ACCOMPANIED THEM.

SOMEHOW, THEY HAD DONE IT. LLEWELLYN HAD ASSERTED HIS WILL. HIS PLACE AS THE CLAN LEADER WOULD NEVER BE QUESTIONED AGAIN.

HE CARRIED HER ALL THE WAY UP THE STAIRS UNTIL THEY REACHED HER BEDROOM. ONCE THERE, HE SET HER DOWN GENTLY, HER NAKED FORM LYING STARKLY AGAINST THE SATIN SHEETS.

"DID I DO OK?" SHE ASKED WITH A PLAYFUL SMILE ON HER FACE.

"YOU WERE PERFECT," HE SAID GENTLY. "THEY TOOK TO YOU IMMEDIATELY."

"HOW DO YOU KNOW?" SHE ASKED.

"BECAUSE THEY DIDN'T TRY TO KILL YOU," HE SAID. "IT WAS CLEAR AS SOON AS YOU ENTERED, ALMOST EVERY MAN IN THAT CIRCLE WANTED YOU. ALL THOUGHTS OF SPILLING YOUR BLOOD FOR OWAIN'S DEATH DISAPPEARED THE MOMENT THEY SAW YOU."

"I BET THEY WEREN'T TOO HAPPY WHEN THEY FOUND OUT THEY WOULDN'T GET TO HAVE ME," SHE SAID.

"THEY'LL LIVE WITH IT," HE SAID. "IF THEY DON'T...THEY KNOW THE CONSEQUENCES OF UPSETTING THE CLAN LEADER."

HE BENT DOWN AND, ONCE MORE KISSED HER LIPS. LOOKING AT HER NOW, STRETCHED OUT AND NAKED AND VULNERABLE, HE COULD HARDLY BELIEVE THAT SHE WAS HIS. THAT THIS BEAUTIFUL WOMAN WOULD BELONG TO NO ONE BUT HIM FROM NOW ON.

"SO, WHAT HAPPENS NOW?" SHE ASKED.

"NOW," HE SAID REMOVING HIS TROUSERS AND JOINING HER ON THE BED. "I GET TO TAKE MY WIFE WITHOUT AN AUDIENCE."

"SOUNDS GOOD TO ME," SHE SAID WITH A SMILE.

AND, AS HER HUSBAND MOVED AGAINST HER. AS HE KISSED, TOUCHED WORSHIPED EVERY INCH OF HER BODY, ALANA KNEW THAT, AT LAST, SHE HAD FOUND HOME.

www.ingramcontent.com/pod-product-compliance
Lightning Source LLC
LaVergne TN
LVHW041642070526
838199LV00053B/3514